THE
FIRST
CHILD

Written and illustrated by
Rosemary Wells

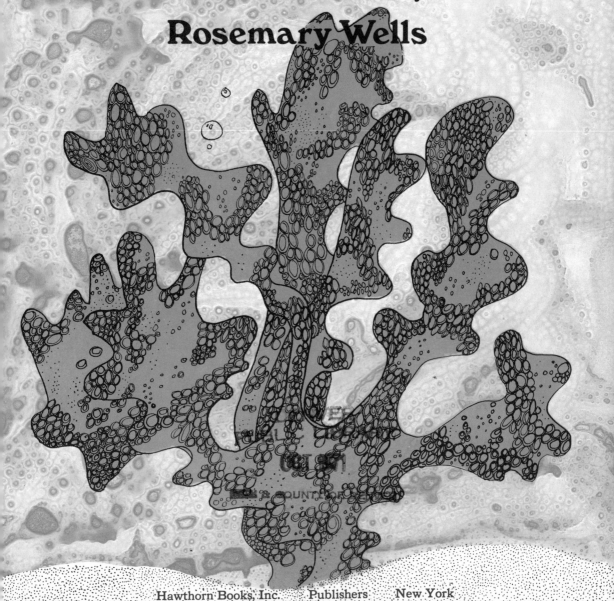

Hawthorn Books, Inc.   Publishers   New York

jW 4687+i

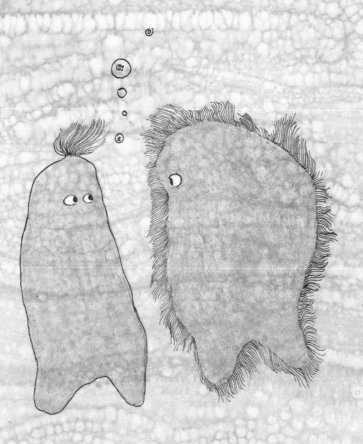

"My feet hurt," said the First Father
to the First Mother. "Do something about it!"
"Oh bother," snapped the First Mother.
"I'm right in the middle of sea-sweeping,
go ask that son of ours if he can help you."

So the First Father went to the First Child.
"Son," he said, "my feet hurt. Do something about it."
"Well, Father," said the First Child politely,
"if you let me wander in the great ocean,
maybe I can find you a pedicure."

"I heard that," said the First Mother, "and
the answer is, No, you're much too young."
The First Child floated over to his mother.

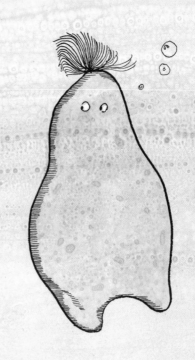

"Mother," he said, "if you let me go, I promise
I'll be home before dark, and I promise I'll make
you the proudest mother that ever could be."

The First Father muttered, "this isn't the time or
place to ask your mother questions." But it was too late.
"Go ask your father," said the First Mother.

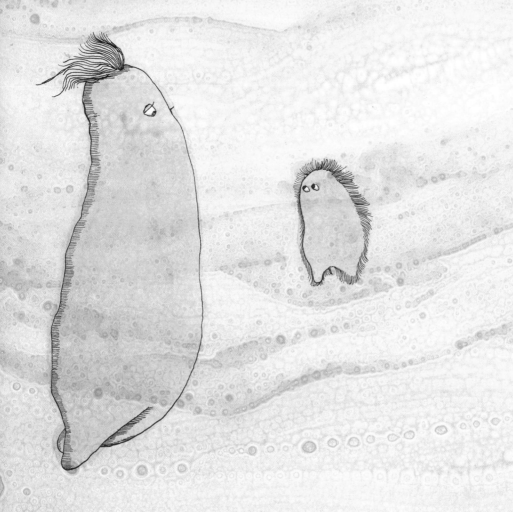

"Far be it from me to start a family argument,"
sighed the First Father.

So the First Child floated away to find a pedicure.

The first thing he came to was a plant, all slimy and wavely.

"I wish I could go faster," he said aloud.

"All children want to go faster," said the plant, waving its thirteen rubbery tendrils around in the water. "Why don't you swim?"

"What's that?" asked the First Child.

"Wiggle your middle and kick with your feet, of course," said the plant.

"Can you help me find a pedicure before dark?" asked the First Child.

"One thing at a time," said the plant.

So the First Child tried.

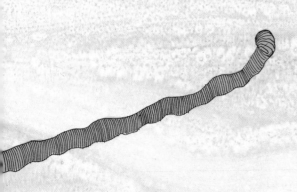

And before you could say "Mustapha Kemal,"
the First Child had become the First Fish.
   "Now can you help me find a pedicure?" he asked
the plant.
   But it only said, "I'm tired," and went
promptly to sleep.

The First Child looked around.
He was horrified!
The ocean was filling up
with the First Octopus, the First Crab,
the First Viperfish,
the First Skate,
the First Electric Eel,
and worst of all, the First Shark!
"They'll gobble me up," he said.

So he poked his head above the water.

There was a tree fern on the beach.

"I wish I could get out of the water,"
he said aloud.

"Why don't you crawl out?" asked the tree fern.

"What's that?" asked the First Child.

"Put one fin ahead of the other, of course," said
the tree fern, waving its razor-sharp fronds
in the air.

"Will you be able to help me find a pedicure
before dark?" asked the First Child.

"One thing at a time," said the tree fern.

So the First Child tried.

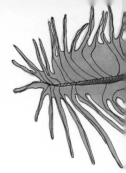

And before you could sing "Cockles and Mussels
Alive, Alive-O," he became the First Turtle.

"Now can you help me find a pedicure before dark?"
he asked the tree fern.

But the tree fern was already dozing off.

The First Child looked around. He was horrified!
The beach was filling up with the First Iguana,
the First Crocodile, the First Alligator, the First Flying Dragon,
the First Gila Monster, the First Dinosaur, but worst of all,
the First Serpent!
"They'll gobble me up!" he said to himself.

He turned around, and now there was a forest behind him. "I wish I could hide in a tree," he said aloud.

"Why don't you climb one?" suggested a flower.

"What's that?" asked the First Child. He thought he knew but he wasn't sure.

"Hang from the branches and swing from your tail, of course," the flower answered.

"Can you help me find a pedicure before dark?" asked the First Child.

"One thing at a time," said the flower.

So the First Child tried.

And before you could dance the tarantella, the
First Child became the First Monkey.

"Now can you help me find a pedicure?" he asked.
But the flower had folded its petals and said no more.

Once again the First Child looked around
and was horrified.

The forest was filling up with the First
Mammoth, the First Boar, the First Tapir,
the First Shrew, but worst of all, the First
Saber-toothed Tiger!

There was nowhere else to go,
and it was getting dark.

The First Child began to cry.

"I'll never find a pedicure now," he said, "and
these creatures will never let me out of this forest."

"Why don't you try thinking?" said the rock
he was sitting on.

"What's thinking?" asked the First Child.

"Use your head, of course," said the rock.

So the First Child tried.

And before you could find a pig in a poke he became the First Boy.

"What do I do now?" he asked. But he found he could answer his own question.

He picked up a rock and threw it at the creatures so that they wouldn't bother him.

Then he shouted, "Mother, I'm home!"

"You're late!" said his mother. "And your
supper is cold."

"My feet still hurt," said his father,
"and I bet you forgot the pedicure, too."

"I have an idea," said the First Child.

"Well, it better be quick," said
his mother.

"And it better be good," said
his father.

"Why don't you soak your feet in the
sea?" suggested the First Child.

So the First Father tried.
And before long his feet felt ever so
much better. And you'd be surprised how
proud the First Mother was!